Book Five:
Shark Camp

With thanks to Paul Ebbs

A TEMPLAR BOOK

First published in the UK in 2014 by Templar Publishing,
an imprint of The Templar Company Limited,
Deepdene Lodge, Deepdene Avenue,
Dorking, Surrey, RH5 4AT, UK
www.templarco.co.uk

www.harry-hammer.co.uk

First edition

ISBN 978-1-84877-925-9

Printed and bound by CPI Group (UK) Ltd,
Croydon, CRO 4YY

Shark Camp

by DAVY OCEAN

Illustrated by Aaron Blecha

templar

Chapter 1

“Daaaaaaaaaaaaaaaaaaaaaaaaaad!
Get your fin-pit OUT OF MY FACE!!!!!!!”

I’m trying to see past my dad’s stinky fin-pit down into the Olimpet Stadium, where the final race of the Underwater Olimpets is about to take place. And where Turbo Tex, the fastest shark in the

ocean, is about to try to win his fifth gold medal of the games!

I squeeze my hammer-head under Dad's pit so I can look down into the massive whalebone-and-coral arena.

All of Shark Point is here. The arena is filled with colour and noise. Some of the sharkletes are limbering up by the track but one is missing. Yes! I haven't missed his entrance.

"Harry!" Dad squirms as I push past him. "Y-y-your dorsal is tickling me!"

Dad – Hugo Hammer, or Mayor Hugo Hammer, as he's known to the rest of Shark Point – starts giggling and twisting. He bumps into my mum and the huge box of Weedpops she's bought for me goes flying up above our heads. Me, Ralph (my pilot-fish pal) and Joe (my jellyfish mate) watch, open-mouthed, as it gets caught in the currents caused by the crowd and floats away.

"I was really looking forward to picking those out from between your teeth!" Ralph whines. (Ralph's a pilot

fish, which means he eats his food from out of sharks' mouths. My mouth in particular.)

I shush Ralph with my fin and try to spot my new hero.

I still like my old hero, Gregor the Gnasher, but he's retired from wrestling and making films and gone to work as an ambassador for the UN (the Underwater Nations). So he's hardly on jellyfishion any more – only the news. And who watches the news?

But since the Olimpets started and tiger shark Turbo Tex came along I haven't really cared. Tex is great because...

1. Tiger sharks are fast and totally scary. Their stripes make them super camouflaged in the water, so they're the best hunters.

2. Turbo Tex is the fastest, scariest and strongest of the lot. The best sharklete in the whole ocean. Scarier than a mum who's just found out you've shoved everything under your bed

instead of tidying 'properly'. Yes. THAT scary.

3. Tex does the TIGER TURBO (more on this in a bit and you'll see exactly how cool it is).
4. He's so fast he's already won the 100 and 800 fathoms in these Olimpet Games. Probably because he doesn't have a stupid hammery head to slow him down like me.

Basically, Turbo Tex is so cool you could use him to make icebergs.

The crowd goes wild as the announcer clears his throat loudly and starts speaking.

"And now, in lane six, the winner of gold medals in the 100 and 800 fathoms, the gold medallist and new world-record

holder in the long dive and triple pike, it's the one, the only, the very stripy TURBO TEX!"

I stretch my hammer-head as far as it will go to see Tex coming down the tunnel onto the swimming track. He's being pulled on a huge clamshell by three beautiful dolphin girls. He waves to the crowd then, with a wink, he swims off the shell. He's going to throw his signature move – THE TIGER TURBO! (See number 4 in my list.)

BOooOM! Tex disappears in an explosion of bubbles as he begins to barrel roll like an out-of-control

washing machine. He spins on the spot with precision power as a white whirlpool of water builds around him, then – WOWSERS! The bubbles from the whirlpool come together to form a giant T. Tex stops dead in front of it with a huge toothy smile on his pointy, stripy face.

The crowd goes even wilder. Mum and Dad are out of their seats,

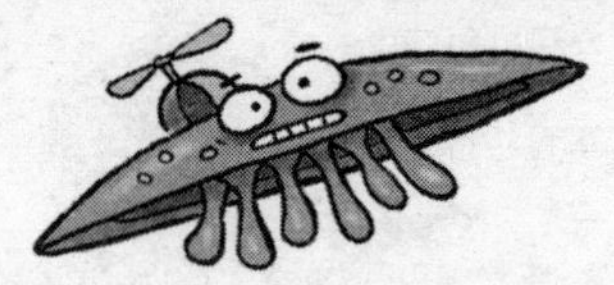

cheering like crazy. I can't imagine how excited everyone will be if Tex actually wins the turtle-hurdles.

Tex takes his place on the track and fits his fins into the starting blocks. The turtle-hurdles look huge but the other sharks in the race seem to be more interested in Tex. Their eyes bulge as Tex flexes his tail and sets his nose at the right angle to get the best kick for the first bend.

BANG! The bullet mackerel is fired by the starting octopus. The race is on!

Tex is first out of the blocks, kicking away with a whoosh of his tail.

The bramble shark in the next lane is blinded by the bubbles and shoots off sideways. The crowd gasps as he crashes into a group of school-squids on a visit

to the stadium with their teacher. The squids are sent flying in all directions. The bramble shark bounces off a row of seats and Tex is waaaaaaay in the lead as he jumps the first turtle-hurdle.

Tex powers round the first bend. In second place, a sleek cookie-cutter shark kicks and kicks, trying to make up the distance to Tex. But he's nowhere near as powerful as the speeding tiger.

WHAM! Tex takes the next turtle and turns his head sideways so that the electric-eel

photographers can
get the best picture of
him with their flashguns.

On the home straight now, Tex throws in a shorter, moving version of the Tiger Turbo. Behind him a longnose spurdog from the South Pacific swims off with an injured fin.

Tex, now knowing that he can't be beaten, jumps the next turtle upside down and swimming with only one fin!

At the last corner, the three other sharks still in the race – the cookie-

cutter, a velvet dogfish and a gulper shark – can only fight not to come last. Tex powers on, kicking and turning and whirring so that the current moves into the crowd and flutters all the flags and banners! The noise is incredible because:

1. Dad is screaming!
2. Mum is screaming!
3. Ralph is screaming!
4. I'm screaming!
5. Joe is hiding from all the screaming!

As Tex crosses the finish line, there are a million electric-eel flashes and a roar that threatens to send a tsunami across the surface of the ocean.

"Mayor coming through! Mayor coming through!" Dad shouts as he starts shouldering his way through the crowd, not even bothering to wait for the other sharks to finish the race. I quickly swim after him. Dad flashes his mayor's chain at the security crabs guarding the track

and they scuttle apart to let us past.

Usually I hate it that Dad is Mayor of Shark Point. He normally wears silly bow ties and waistcoats, and he makes terrible jokes whenever he's giving a speech. But right now, being the mayor's son seems like the coolest thing in the world because Dad is heading straight for Turbo Tex!

Tex is waving to the crowd, and has his five medals hanging round his neck. Dad pushes up to him, takes him by the fin and pumps it up and down about a thousand times.

"Mr Turbo, can I say that was the

most exciting race
I've ever seen,"
he gushes.

Tex
looks down
at Dad.
"Yes, you
can say it."
Tex winks at me then turns back to Dad.
"Go on, then."

Dad frowns, not really getting the joke, so I nudge him in the side. "Say it again, Dad."

"Oh. That was the most excit—"

Tex laughs and slaps Dad on the

shoulder with a big, meaty fin. "Only joking, dude. You the mayor of this town?"

Dad nods. "I certainly am, and can I just say how honoured—"

Tex slaps Dad on the shoulder and winks at me again. "I guess this little fella must be your boy, then?"

Dad nods again. "Yes, that's Harry, and as I was saying—"

Tex goes to slap Dad on the shoulder yet again, but Dad has learnt his lesson and backs off. Tex sees that I'm holding out my autograph book and a cuttlefish pen. He reaches down and signs his name right across two pages. "I'm way

too big to fit on one page, kid!" he says with a grin.

Coolest. Thing. EVER!

My smile's so big it's threatening to split my hammer in two.

"Get your phone, Mr Mayor," Tex tells Dad.

Nodding and trying hard not to open his mouth again, Dad reaches for his SeaBerry.

Tex spins me around to face Dad and flops his fin around me.

"Smile wide, kid!"

But before I can open my mouth...

FLUBBBBBBBBBBBBBEEEERRRRRR!!!!

The world shakes and my eyes start rattling in my head. I hear Rick Reef snickering as the camera on Dad's SeaBerry flashes.

When my stupid rubbery head finally stops vibrating, Rick Reef and Donny Dogfish come into focus. Rick is holding his belly and laughing hard. He's always flubbering my head with his fin. He thinks it's hilarious, and so does his sidekick Donny, who is wiping tears of laughter from his eyes.

I look about wildly for Tex, but he's already swimming off with his fins draped around the pretty dolphin girls.

"Oh," says Dad, looking at his phone.

"Did you get the picture?" I ask, swimming over to take a look.

"Well... sort of..."

My heart sinks as I look at the screen.

Rick flubbered me just before Dad took the picture. Tex is smiling and waving – NEXT TO A HAMMERHEAD-SHAPED BLUR!!!!

Outside the Olimpet Stadium, I kick empty Weedpop boxes along the ground as the crowd streams around us. Ralph and Joe are doing everything they can to cheer me up, but it isn't working. All

I can think about is my stupid flubbery head, and Rick ruining what was probably the only chance I'll ever have to get my picture taken with a superstar.

I kick another empty box, and huff like a sea-cow doing a sea-cowpat.

BOING!!!!

For a moment, I think that Rick's come back and flubbered my head again. But when I look up I see that I've bashed into someone. Someone wearing a bright red cap and scarf and a whalebone woggle.

"Look where you're going, boy!" a voice booms.

My heart sinks. The voice belongs to Drago Dogfish, leader of the Shark Point Cub Pack, and dad of Rick's sidekick Donny!

"**Attennnnnnnnnnnnshun!**"

bellows Drago, straightening his woggle and pushing back his cap with a pointy fin. "Have you seen Donny? He should be busy getting

ready for camp tomorrow – as should all of you!"

In the excitement over Turbo Tex, I'd forgotten we're off to Cub Camp tomorrow. If my heart sinks any further, I'm going to have to dig it out of the seabed.

Drago glares at us. Joe starts to **pop, pop, pop** from his bottom, and Ralph tries to hide in my mouth.

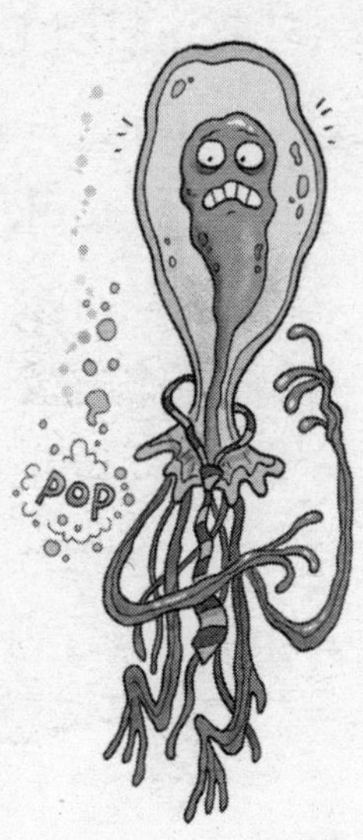

"I just asked you a question!" Drago barks. "Tell me – what are you supposed to do when

someone asks you a question?"

"We have to answer, sir," I say.

Drago shakes his head.

I look at Ralph and Joe. They look as baffled as me.

"You don't just have to answer. You have to give THE VERY BEST ANSWER POSSIBLE!" Drago says. Then he stares at me. "Go on, then."

I look at him blankly. "What?"

"Give me your VERY BEST ANSWER POSSIBLE."

I point back to the stadium with one end of my hammer. "I – er – think Donny's still in there with Rick, sir."

I'm not sure if that's the very best answer possible but thankfully Drago starts to smile. "I see," he says. "I bet he's checking out the equipment and preparing for ALL THE AWESOME RACES AND SPORTING CHALLENGES I've got planned for you boys at camp."

No, I think to myself. He's probably up to no good with Rick, looking for poor, unsuspecting hammerheads to flubber just when they're having the MOST IMPORTANT PHOTOGRAPHS OF THEIR LIVES TAKEN!

But of course I don't say it.

"Ah, that Donny, he's a chip off the

old block," Drago says. "Always thinking ahead. ALWAYS DOING HIS BEST. Not like you lot, slouching home when you could still be in the Olimpet Stadium learning things. You'll never amount to anything with that kind of attitude, lads. You won't be winners like my boy Donny. You'll be losers! Is that what you want? NO! No, it isn't! Life is about pushing yourself to the limit, not popping from your bottom, hiding behind someone else's teeth or failing to look where you're going! Do I make myself clear?"

Me, Ralph and Joe nod.

Well, Joe bottom-pops again, but he

has a good go at nodding too.

"Right! I expect to see you three bright and early tomorrow morning. I have plans for you all. PLANS!"

Drago pulls himself up into a salute, straightens his woggle again, then swims

off towards the stadium.

I slump to the seabed. "Just when you think the day can't get any worse, it does," I say.

Ralph and Joe agree. Not one of us is looking forward to two days of being yelled at to DO OUR BEST by Drago Dogfish.

I look up, hoping to see something – anything – to make me feel better. But all I see is a huge picture of Turbo Tex looking down at me with enormous eyes and sparkly teeth.

If only I was a supreme sharklete like Tex. Then everyone would love me

and Drago wouldn't shout at me and Rick wouldn't dare flubber my head.

But the fact is, I'm just a boyshark with a stupid head shaped like a hammer. Tex is a winner and I'm a loser.

In fact, the only Olimpet gold medal I could win right now is the one for Most Flubbery Head in the World!

Chapter 2

I look around the room. Humphrey, my humming-fish alarm clock, is still fast asleep. If I've woken up before he's gone off I must be nervous. I'd already set him earlier than usual so I had time to get ready for camp.

At the thought of camp, I swim

straight out of bed. If I want to be a sharklete like Turbo Tex I need to start training pronto. Plus I really need to get in shape for whatever Drago has planned. I know I've left it a bit late – but a quick workout has got to be better than nothing.

I think back to the sharkletes limbering up and stretching in the Olimpet Stadium before their race. I try warming up my tail.

It stays cold.

I start stretching out my fins.

They stay stiff.

I begin rolling my hammer.

It wobbles and flubbers all by itself.

Great!

Drago's voice drifts back into my mind. "You won't be winners like my boy Donny! You'll be losers! Is that what you want? NO! No, it isn't! Life is about pushing yourself to the limit!"

Well, if pushing yourself to the limit is what's needed then it's time to PUSH!

1. I start with sit-ups. Hup! Hup! Hup! (Ouch! Ouch! Ouch!)
2. Move on to dorsal jumps. Flap! Flap! Flap! (Ache! Ache! Ache!)
3. Start fifty fin-presses. I manage two. (Twinge! Twinge!)

4. Roll for a sequence of hammer jerks. (Flub! Flub! Flubber!)
5. Leap high for a toothy jaw snarkle.

CRAAAAAAAASSSSSSSSHHHHH!!!!

My out-of-control flubbery hammer bounces into Lenny the Lantern Fish, who immediately floods the room with light and...

HMMMMMMMMMMMMMM!!!

HMMMMMMMMMMMMMMMM!!!

Humphrey wakes up in panic and starts his alarm humming on the loudest possible setting!

My next bit of exercise is chasing them both around the room, trying to turn Lenny off and stop Humphrey from humming so loudly he wakes Mum and Dad.

When I finally catch them, I see that Humphrey is not at all happy.

"It's my job to wake everyone up!" he moans. "I'm a humming-fish alarm clock, that's what I do!" He turns and glares at Lenny. "Are you trying to put me out of a job?"

Then Lenny gets angry too. "It wasn't my fault!" He points at me. "It was him! He flubbered me sideways and I panicked!"

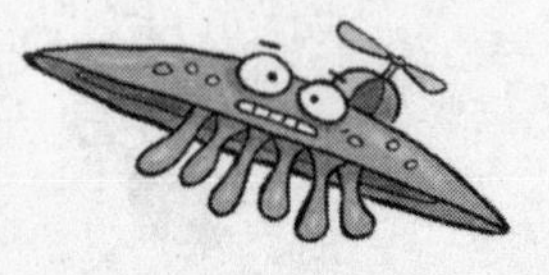

Lenny and Humphrey glare at me.

"That's what you have to do if you want to be a winner," I say. "Push yourself to the limit!"

"Any more of that," says Humphrey, "and we'll push you down a whirlpool!"

"Sorry!" I say, as I have another idea. "Look, I need your help. I'm trying to get fit for Cub Camp today. I need you two to be turtle-hurdles."

They both look at me like I've gone mad. But they don't understand. Turbo Tex didn't win the Olimpet turtle-hurdles (on his back, with just the one fin) without a lot of practice.

I place Humphrey and Lenny equal distances apart in my bedroom: Humphrey on my seaweed blanket and Lenny next to my flaptop, and then...

WHOOSH, I'm off! Zooming around the room, kicking with my tail, and...

LEAP!!! I'm over Humphrey!

ZOOM!!! I'm coming round my seabed!

LEAP!!! I'm over Lenny!!!

ZOOOM!!! And I'm coming around again!

This is brilliant! At last something is going right!!!

LEAP!!! And I'm...

SMASHING!!! into Mum as she floats through the door with a tray of breakfast...

I hit her fins so hard that the tray spins out of control, turning the bowl of prawn-flakes out all over my seabed.

Breakfast in bed has become breakfast on bed.

I look at Mum.

Mum looks at me.

She is not happy.

Neither are Lenny and Humphrey, who have also been splattered with prawn-flakes.

"I've got breakfast all over my

lantern," Lenny grumbles as he swims back to his shelf.

"I'm a humming-fish alarm clock, not a humming-fish hurdle!" Humphrey hisses as he swims back to my bedside table.

"Harry! You silly boy!" Mum says. "There isn't any time for playing. You've got to get ready for camp."

"I'm not playing, I'm training!" I reply crossly.

Hmmm – I bet Turbo Tex doesn't have to put up with this kind of thing.

Mum is unusually quiet as we swim down to the coach for camp. Normally, when we swim anywhere she likes singing one of her terrible songs, but her mouth is shut tight, and her hammer is looking straight ahead. Perhaps she still hasn't forgiven me for wrecking breakfast.

Loads of other parents and kids are at the whalecoach by the time we get there. The coach is filling up. The whale underneath is yawning and looking really bored. Ralph and Joe are aboard already and waving at me from one of the windows.

I turn to Mum to say goodbye, and that's when the most embarrassing thing that has ever happened to anyone ever in the history of seaworld happens.

She starts to cry!

Then she pulls me close and wraps her fins around me – in front of everyone!

"I can't believe my little starfish is going away for two whole days!" she sobs. Then she eases her grip on me and turns around. "You will look after him, won't you, Drago?"

I go bright pink from the top of my hammer to the flukes of my tail. I peek one end of my hammer out from under Mum's fin. Drago is floating at the entrance to the whalecoach with his clipboard, ticking off names. Right next to him, just about to burst out laughing, are Donny and Rick.

"Don't worry, Mrs Hammer, your little starfish will be safe with me," says Drago as he ticks off my name.

"Muuuuuuuuuuuummmmmm! Let go!" I whisper, hoping that no one else is looking. But of course they are. When I glance up at the coach I see noses and eyes and sonar pods pressed against every window.

"Ah, mummy's lickle baby," Rick sneers gleefully. "Mummy's lickle ickle baby who should be tucked up in a pram. We should rename you Harry PRAMmer!"

I can even see a smile creeping across Drago's mouth as he shoos

Rick and Donny on to the whalecoach. "Enough of that, boys. I won't stand for any nonsense. Not on my watch."

I finally manage to wriggle out of Mum's clutches just as she tries to plant a slobbery kiss on my hammer. I drag my rucksack onto my back and dart on to the coach, as Mum waves and cries.

Things don't get any better on the coach. Mum held on to me for so long, there are hardly any seats left. Rick and Donny are at the back, making faces out of the window. Ralph and Joe are about halfway down. I start to make my way along the aisle towards them, but a fin

grabs my shoulder and spins me around.

"Not so fast, boy!" booms Drago. "Your mum's made me promise to keep a special eye on you, so that's exactly what I'm going to do!"

I want a freak sea current to whoosh on to the coach and wash me straight back off again.

Drago sits me down in the seat next to him, and makes a great show of doing up my seat belt.

From the back I can hear Donny and Rick start to sing, "Pram, pram, bring him a pram..."

A ripple of giggles runs up the

whalecoach. I bury my hammer in my fins and start making a list of how rubbish camp is going to be to try to drown out the song.

1. Trapped for two whole days with Rick and Donny.

"Pram! Pram!"

2. Made to look like a complete and utter loser by Drago.

"Bring him a pram!"

3. Everyone laughing behind their fins at me (to be honest this has started already, I can see them now).

"Harry's mum boo hoos!"

4. And this song following me wherever I go!

"And hugs like a clam!"

See what I mean?

I sink into the seat and cover my ears.

But then I see something that makes me sit up straighter than a ship's mast.

A tiger shark is getting on the coach. A tiger shark just like Turbo Tex!

Well, he's only a kid shark like me, but he's a real tiger shark! He swims up the coach, not making eye contact with anyone (waaaay cool), carrying a stripy rucksack that matches the stripes down his side.

"This is Tony," Drago calls out,

making a note on his clipboard. "His family have just moved to Shark Point and he'll be joining us at camp." Drago turns to Tony. "I'm expecting GREAT things from you, boy!"

Tony swims slowly past Drago. The

other kids stop singing and watch. I can hear Rick whistling through his teeth tunelessly because he's no longer the centre of attention.

Suddenly I have a plan. A great, magnificent and awesome plan.

1. I'll make friends with Tony Tiger.
2. I'll get him to teach me how to become a supreme sharklete.
3. Then I'll be faster than the others and win ALL the races.
4. This will shut Rick and Donny up for good!
5. And I'll have the best time EVER!

Chapter 3

The Sea-cub Camp is located many leagues away in the Frondy Forest. After a few hours, we head into the sea cliffs. The whalecoach starts driving through narrow passages and ravines, kicking its flukes slowly so it doesn't dislodge any rocks. Slimy strands of seaweed form a

gloomy tunnel of brown above us.

But I can hardly concentrate on the journey because I can't take my eyes off Tony Tiger. He doesn't look at me, but then he doesn't look at anyone. Far too cool for that, I reckon.

When we get to the camp, it's a relief to be out in the light, but the forest of huge brown and black weeds still surrounds us on all sides.

Drago gets us out of the coach. I try to float as close as I can to Tony, but he doesn't seem to notice me at all. I wonder if he heard Rick and Donny's song about me.

A piercing shriek rings out, making us all jump. Drago is wearing a whalebone whistle around his neck and he's blowing it so hard it's making his eyes even gogglier than mine.

We all quickly get into line, floating as straight as we can. Drago stops blowing his whistle and starts swimming up and down in front of us.

"You know what time it is," he says. "And I know what time it is."

We all look at him blankly.

"Five past twelve?" Joe says nervously.

Drago blows his whistle crossly. "**NO! NO! NO!** It's time for the Sea-cub Motto!"

We all pull ourselves up as straight as we can and use our loudest voices. "I promise that I will do my best," we say.

"**NO! NO! NO! NO! NO!**" Drago yells. "I've changed the words. From now on, our motto is: I promise that I won't do my best— "

We all stare at him.

"I promise that I will do **BETTER THAN MY VERY MOST ALL-TIME BEST!**" Drago bellows.

Hmmm, it doesn't flow quite as smoothly as the original motto – especially when we try it.

"I... promise... very... than... better... most... best... all-time..." we stammer, apart from Tiger Kid, who says nothing. He really is Cool. As. Ice.

Drago sighs. "Okay, enough of that. It's time to GET DOWN TO BUSINESS! THE BUSINESS OF BEING THE BEST!" He starts swimming round and round in a circle. "This camp will push you TO

THE LIMIT. It will test you TO THE MAX." He swims faster and faster. I'm starting to get dizzy just watching him. "It will… it will…" Drago stops swimming and crashes into Donny.

"Dad!" Donny says, looking embarrassed.

"Sorry, son. Got hit by a – er – freak current." Drago quickly straightens his cap. "Anyway, as I was about to say, by the time we get to the COMPETITION tomorrow you're all going to be working together as a team." He looks at us and narrows his eyes. "And remember, there is no 'I' IN TEAM!"

Yes, but there is a 'U' in dumbo, I think. I don't say it out loud.

"Right, time for the first exercise," Drago says. "Putting your tents up. The last one to get his done will have to drop and give me fifty!"

None of us dare ask him fifty what.

Luckily, I'm one of the first to get my tent up. This is mainly because I don't need to borrow a hammer to knock in the tent pegs. I just use the side of my head.

I look about. Rick and Donny are sword-fighting with their tent poles. Ralph is trying to find Joe – who is hiding from an octokid swinging six hammers at once.

Tony Tiger's trying to get his tent up, but doesn't seem to be making a good job of it. I bet it's because he's too cool to ever go camping. Then I realise that this is a perfect opportunity to put my plan into action.

"All right, Tony? I'm Harry," I say, swimming over. "Do you need some help?"

Tony looks away.

Man, I must be so uncool he doesn't even want to be seen talking to me in case he loses his seacred.

I decide to try again and swim round to face Tony. "My head's pretty good at putting up tents. Look..."

I bang in a couple of pegs to show him, and get the back end of his tent up. Tony just floats there, his ace stripes glistening in the light. He even looks fast standing still.

I just look like a hammer with a tail.

I try a joke. "Are those go-faster stripes?" I say, pointing at his side.

Tony just looks at me like I'm

something your fin might slide in.

Great.

I swim about quickly putting up Tony's tent, not bothering to say anything more.

"Time's up!" Drago yells, just as I finish.

Rick is next to his tent, but Donny is nowhere to be seen. Then I notice his tail sticking out under the tent flap. He's holding it up from the inside to make it look like they've finished. Cheats!

Ralph and Joe are still trying to get their final tent peg in. Joe has turned bright red from the effort.

"Right, Ralph and Joe drop and give me fifty!" Drago bellows.

"Fifty what?" asks Joe.

"Farty-pops," sniggers Rick, flicking the flap of his tent to cover Donny's tail.

"FIN-PRESSES!" yells Drago.

Ralph and Joe begin...

Press, press, press.

Pop, pop,

poppity-pop.

When Ralph and Joe have finally finished, Drago leads us all into the Frondy Forest. The weed-trunks are huge and dark, and wide leaves sweep backwards and forwards in the slow currents. Dark little fish dart in the hollows and strange rustles in the undergrowth make us look this way and that.

It's all a bit creepy.

Drago leads us into another, smaller clearing. "Right, you lot, it's time for the real work to begin! Welcome to THE BEST ASSAULT COURSE THE UNDERWATER WORLD HAS EVER SEEN!"

As my eyes adjust to the brightness, I see what he's talking about and my stomach does several flips.

The assault course is a huge collection of spinning wheels, tiny squeeze gaps, purse-neck nets, and water-powered whirring tentacles. We all stand open-mouthed as Drago takes us through each piece of equipment.

“Cubs, your first test is to see if you can get around the course without being spun out of the wheel, stuck in a hole, tangled in the nets, or captured by the tentacles.”

We all look at each other in shocked silence.

Drago clicks his stopwatch and starts sending us off one at a time. I'm in the middle of the pack – in front of Tony, but just behind Rick and Donny.

"Go on, Donny, show 'em how it's done!" shouts Drago as he sends his son off, with Rick following fifteen seconds later.

Then it's my turn. I look back at Tony. Maybe if I can get through the course in a good time, he won't think I'm such a hammery rubberhead and he'll want to be my friend. I was stupid thinking that

putting up the tent would impress him. He'll be much more impressed if I can show him some sharklete skills.

It all goes well at first. I zip through the purse-nets, avoid the tentacles, and slip through all the gaps in the rocks. I'm doing so well, I'm catching up with Rick and Donny. I really hope Tony is watching.

I kick away from the rocks and head towards the spinning wheel. It looks like the paddle from a sunken leggy air-breather's pleasure boat. Strands of seaweed are stuck to its white wooden slats. They whip around as it turns on the current.

Donny has ducked below the wheel to avoid it. Luckily for him, Drago doesn't notice. He's too busy clicking his stopwatch as he sends Tony off. Rick dives between two slats and makes it to the centre of the wheel. He hangs on to the hub with a fin as he tries to get the timing right to dart through the slats on the other side.

As I get closer he looks at me and smirks. "Here's Harry Prammer!"

I ignore him – it's not Rick I'm interested in. I sneak a look back at Tony as I dive towards the wheel. Rick kicks, narrowly making it out between the slats

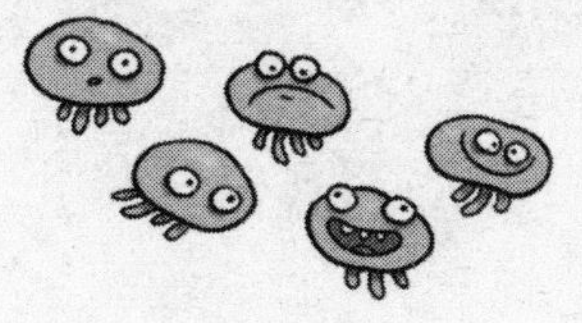

as it spins round and round.

This is when I realise it was a mistake ignoring Rick. He wasn't just waiting for the right time to swim out between the whirring slats, he was laying a trap for me!

Rick has pulled a long strand of seaweed into the centre of the wheel and looped it around. And now, instead of being a good place to hang on to while I wait for the wheel to rotate, it's all slippery! As I desperately try to hang on to the hub, I slide straight off, bounce into the slats and get tangled in the seaweed fronds hanging there.

Upside down!
I go round and
round and round
and round and round
(I'm gonna be sick!)
and round and round
and round (I am sick!)
and round and round and
round. I see Tony
slipping
easily
into the
wheel and
out the
other side.

He completely ignores my embarrassed wave through the cloud of prawn-flakes I had for breakfast.

Once the wheel has stopped, it takes three hours for a very unhappy Drago to untangle me from the seaweed.

By that time, everyone else is back at camp, and I can hear them all singing. (“Sick, sick, Harry’s been sick! The wheel turned him about and his breakfast flew out!”)

Really – could this camp get any worse?

Chapter 4

As soon as I get back to camp I go and hide in my tent until the singing stops. Ralph and Joe ask if I want to come and play finball, but I ignore them. I just want to be alone. But then I smell clamburgers and hotfrogs on the currents washing through my tent and my stomach groans.

I undo the tent flap and swim to where everyone is sitting on rafts of pink sea-sponge, around a small whirlpool.

I spot Ralph and Joe over by Drago, cooking hotfrogs in a handy volcanic vent.

Nothing cheers a shark up more than an approaching meal, so I should be happy, but:

1. No one's talking to me. Mainly, I think, because they don't want to laugh in my face.
2. I can't interrupt Ralph and Joe while they're cooking hotfrogs without getting told off by Drago.
3. I catch sight of myself in a passing mirror-fish and I see that I'm still slightly green

from my time on the wheel.

4. This makes me feel fed up.
5. Very fed up.
6. Totally fed up.

I could go on, but maybe I should have another go trying to make friends with Tony? I scan the cubs gathered around the whirlpool.

Tony is sitting on a sea-pillow with Rick and Donny.

7. I'm now properly, properly, humongously FED UP!!!!!

How can I ever learn to be a great sharklete like Turbo Tex now Tony is mates with my arch-flubberer?

I turn on my tail and gloomily begin to swim back towards my tent, but Drago spots me.

"And where do you think you're going, Harry?" he shouts.

I stop and shrug. "Dunno, sir."

"Well, how about I tell you? You're going to make up for mucking up the assault course by becoming our waiter for the night." Drago hands me a tray of clamburgers. "Off you go."

I take the tray and start doling out clamburgers. Rick and Donny take two each and try to flubber my head, but I manage to duck away. When I've finally served everyone, all that's left for me to eat are two empty clamburger buns and half a hotfrog.

I sit on my own at the back of the circle and chew unhappily on my food. Ralph swims over.

"Any food between your teeth?" he asks.

I shake my head glumly. There's not enough for me, let alone my swimming toothbrush!

"Listen up, everyone," Drago says once we've all finished eating. He's sitting closest to the whirlpool and his head is lit up by a couple of lantern fish. The current in the water is making his scarf waft around his face like the creepy weeds in the forest. "It's time for a ghost story," he

whispers.

Everyone sits forward excitedly, except me. I couldn't care less.

"I want to tell you a tale. A tale of a whale. A tale of doom and a sharp harpoon! Of a moonless night and a terrible fright, and a whaley ghost who's coming here soon!" Drago looks at us all, his face deadly serious. "It was a hundred years ago, I'll have you all know, when Jonah the whale was blown by a gale,

out here to the fronds, to the backs of beyonds, where even leggy air-breathers won't sail!"

I have to admit that I'm starting to get interested in the story. I float a little closer on my sea-sponge.

Drago continues. "Jonah was cold and alone, shivering to the bone, too far from the shore, when he heard the ship roar. A ship of the dead, floating over his head, the captain a spectre, with rotten eyes full of gore!"

I move even closer. The dark water around the whirlpool seems to be closing in. I see Donny's fin reaching out to hold

Rick's. Rick holds on for a moment, then realises what he's doing and slaps it away. Donny starts hugging himself instead.

Drago's voice gets lower and whisperier. "Jonah tried to hide, but he was caught by the tide. He was flung on the beach, and the dead started to screech. The dead captain began a-stabbing, under the light of the moon, with his fearsome harpoon!"

Pop pop pop pop pop poppity pop!

I turn to look at Joe. But for once it wasn't his bottom popping – it was the squid kid, Sammy, floating next to him.

Drago starts drifting over our heads. The lantern fishes are now behind him, making him look like a big black shadow.

"And now it is said, that this whale who is dead, swims through the dark, seeking fishes and sharks, to feast on with glee, for breakfast, lunch AND tea! **ARRRRRRRGGGGGHHHHHH!!!!**"

At this point, the lantern fish go out and everyone screams! Even me!

Drago laughs. "Lights on, boys!"

But nothing happens.

"Lantern fish!" Drago shouts. "I said lights on."

"We are on!" one of the lanterns calls back.

"I'm sorry," Sammy Squid whimpers. "I couldn't help it."

Suddenly I realise what's happened. Sammy has got so scared that he's let out an ink explosion and it's blocking out all the light!

Drago starts swimming about. "Everyone, shake your tails and clear the ink."

We all do as we're told. As the ink

clears, I see Sammy's tentacles totally caught up with Joe's jellyfish legs. It's like they both tried to hug each other to pieces.

The others rush to untangle Sammy and Joe, but I hold back. Not because I don't want to help, but because I've just

been struck by THE BEST IDEA EVER!

I can feel my goggly hammerhead eyes growing wider and wider as I realise how brilliant it is. If I play this right:

1. Everyone will stop singing stupid songs about me.
2. I'll be friends with them all again and
3. I'll be a supreme sharklete just like TURBO TEX!

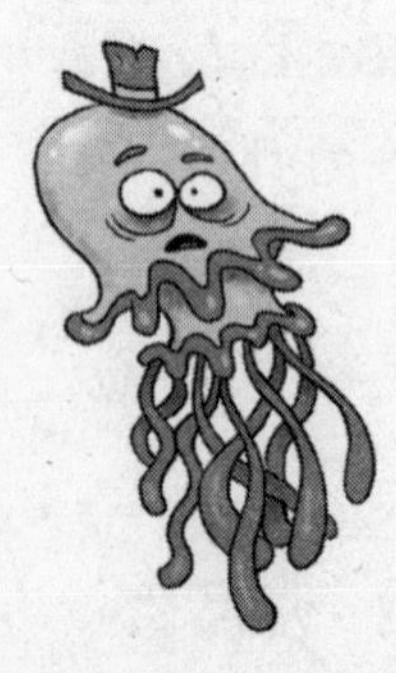

Chapter 5

Drago has sent us all to bed with the order to "DREAM THE DREAMS OF WINNERS!"

Ralph and Joe are in my tent, going on about the midnight feast they've been planning for ages. They're so excited

about it I haven't had a chance to mention my own plan.

"Do we have to stay up until midnight?" asks Joe. "That's way past my bedtime."

"A midnight feast doesn't have to happen at midnight, stupid," says Ralph, eyeing the pile of sweets Joe is pulling out of his rucksack. "It can be held at any time!"

"Then why is it called a midnight feast?" Joe uses several tentacles to lay out the sweets in neat rows in front of him.

"Because... because..." Ralph

scratches his chin with his fin and thinks. But the sight of all the sweets is obviously too distracting for him. "Oh, I dunno! Who cares?! What have we got?"

Joe finishes arranging the sweets. "Okay," he says, floating back to admire his handiwork. "We've got Kit-Katfishes, Double Shipwreckers, Sealion Bars, Maltweedsers, and a huuuuuuge bag of Seasick 'n' Mix."

"Got any Tangfishsticks?" Ralph says hopefully. "I love picking them out from between Harry's teeth."

"Listen," I say, but Ralph's way too busy gazing at the sweets to pay me any attention.

Joe reaches inside his rucksack, and pulls out a brightly coloured bag of Tangfishsticks. "There you go."

"I need to tell you something," I try again.

Ralph grabs the bag, opens it and shoves it in my face. "Start eating, Harry! I want to get to work!"

I push the bag away. "I haven't got

time for a midnight feast!"

"I thought it could be at any time?" says Joe, flashing yellow and purple, like he always does when he's confused. "I don't understand!"

"Just eat a few, Harry," Ralph says. "It won't take long!"

"No, there's something I need to do," I say, brushing past the sweets and heading for the tent flap. "Something way more important than a midnight feast."

They look at me blankly.

"What could be more important than a midnight feast?" Ralph says, his eyes wide.

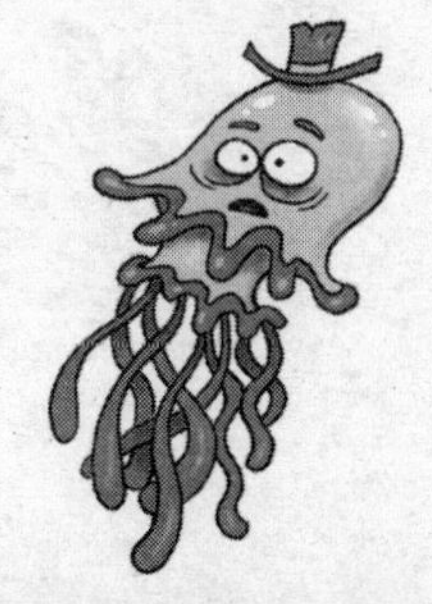

"Come with me, and you'll see," I reply.

"Can I bring the Tangfishsticks?" asks Ralph.

"No!" I hiss, as I open the flap. "Follow me. And keep your voices down."

Outside, the camp is quiet and mostly dark. The lantern fish have gone out and the only light is coming from the moon reflecting on the ocean above.

"D-d-do we have to go?" Joe starts trembling and his jellyfish body flashes red for danger.

"It's too dark and scary!"

I shush him with my fin and swim on.

Suddenly I hear a loud rustling. I spin my goggle eyes wildly.

"Ralph!" I whisper crossly. "I told you not to bring the Tangfishsticks!"

Ralph looks embarrassed and puts the bag back in his pocket.

We swim on through the silent camp, and eventually reach the tent I want. I float up close to it.

"Sammy? Sammy?" I whisper. "It's me, Harry. Are you awake?"

I hear the zip of a sleeping bag being undone inside the tent.

"Well, I am now!"

The flap opens and Sammy Squid sticks out a tentacle, followed by a pair of sleepy eyes. "What do you want?"

"Yes," says Ralph, looking at me, "what do we want?"

"Sammy," I say, ignoring Ralph, "I want you to spray some stripes down my side in ink. I want to look like Turbo Tex. Can you do it?"

"Yes and no," says Sammy.

"I was less confused when we were talking about midnight feasts not being at midnight," Joe mutters. "What do you mean, yes and no?"

"Yes, I can do it, but no, I can't do it now," says Sammy, rubbing his eyes.

I stare at him. "Why not?"

"I can't spray ink unless I'm scared," he replies. "It's a defence mechanism, innit? I need to feel threatened."

I open my mouth and show Sammy my hunter's teeth.

Nothing happens – apart from Ralph trying to dive in for a quick snack.

"Sorry, Harry, but you're just not

scary," Sammy says with a grin. "Not even a little bit."

Great – my plan is falling to pieces because I'm not scary enough to frighten a kid squid. I look about, trying to think. The camp is dark and silent, the currents cold and creepy. In the distance, the leaves of the Frondy Forest move lazily in the water like beckoning fingers. It's very, very spooky.

Yes! Got it!

"Okay... I have another idea," I say. "What if I told you a ghost story like Drago's?"

"No thanks!" says Sammy, backing

into the tent. "One was bad enough!"

"Please, Sammy!" I grab the bag of Tangfishsticks from Ralph's pocket and hold them out to Sammy. "You can have these if you say yes."

"No... mmmmmmmph! He... mmmmmmmph! Can't... mmmmph!" Ralph splutters as I put my fin over his mouth to shut him up. I wave the bag in front of Sammy with my other fin at the same time.

"The whole bag?"

Sammy says, coming forward again.

"Yes. And all the Double Shipwreckers and Maltweedsers we have back in our tent too."

I'm having to hold Ralph down now. He's not happy at all.

Sammy nods. "Okay, I'll do it."

"Great!" I say. "Just make sure you get tiger stripes down both sides of me, right?"

Sammy nods, and curls his bum under his head so it's right in my face.

The things I have to do to save my reputation!

"Right... okay..." I start. But my mind

is completely blank. I don't know any ghost stories! I look about wildly but I can't think of anything. I'm just going to have to make a story up on the spot. It can't be that difficult, can it?

I screw up my eyes and lower my voice to a whisper like Drago. "Here is a tale about a sea ghost, which will scare you so much, it will put you off lunch, and right off... right off... prawn toast!"

Bit of a shaky start, but not too bad. I glance at Sammy. He's looking completely calm. Ralph has a face like a grumpy granddad walrus chewing a spine fish, and Joe is a peaceful shade of blue.

Right, time to step it up a bit. "It's a terrible story, about a squid boy called... er... Rory, who was from somewhere... near to... ummm... Tanglemory?"

I look at the others. Joe is still blue, but Sammy is starting to tremble. Yes, it's working!

"He liked to go out, at night all – ummm – about. To the ship graveyard – even though it was hard... to get there, because his – er – navigation skills were a bit pants."

I frown. I never realised making stuff up could be so difficult!

But Sammy is starting to really

shake now. He's obviously terrified! I'd better carry on. "So, the night of the fright, he went there and – ummm – right, there was a figure in white. Was it a sheet? No – ummm – not quite. Rory did swim away as fast as a ... umm ... very fast thing. " I growl my best sharky growl. "And he never went near there again!"

Sammy is shaking so much he's vibrating the tent. He's scared out of his tentacles!

Except...

1. Sammy isn't terrified. (Not even a little bit.)
2. Sammy is trying not to laugh. (And he's about to fail.)

3. As I finish he can't hold it any longer. (Here he goes.)
4. He starts to laugh, and soon he can't stop. ("Hahahahahahahahaha!!!")
5. Out comes the ink from his bum. (Pfffffffffffffffftttttt!!!)
6. But instead of a stream, it's a spray. (Oh NO!!)
7. And as he laughs more, it covers me. (Stoooooooooooop!!!)
8. Too late. I'm not striped like a tiger shark at all. I'M COVERED IN SPOTS!

Chapter 6

When I wake up the next morning, the first thing I do is check my skin to see if the spots have faded. I can't believe my goggly eyes. The spots look even worse in the daylight. Instead of looking like a really cool tiger shark, I look like a hammer teen with pimples!

"Come on, you lazy lot!" I hear Drago shouting from outside. "Sleeping's for losers and waking's for winners! It's time to do some warming up."

I don't need warming up, I need washing down. I rub at the spots with my hammer. But no matter how hard I rub, they just won't fade. Squid ink is EVIL!

I sigh and swim outside. Drago takes one look at me and throws his fins up in panic.

"Right, everyone – back away from Harry!" He rushes towards me. "I've never seen such a bad case of seasles in my life! Get yourself back to bed while I

call an ambuwhale."

"I don't need an ambuwhale, sir," I say. "I don't have seasles."

"Don't have seasles?" Drago bellows. "Then what in ocean's name do you have?" He eyes me suspiciously. I can't tell him the truth – that would be way too embarrassing. But I have to tell him something. So I tell him a bit of the truth.

"It's a squid fart, sir."

Drago looks as if his eyes are going to burst out of his head. "A what?"

"A squid fart. I made Sammy laugh and he popped all over me. With ink."

All of the cubs start roaring with

laughter. I'll never live this down.

Ever.

Everyone's still laughing at breakfast. Keeping my eyes down, I carry my bowl of prawn-flakes to the very end of the canteen tent and begin to eat. I'm halfway through the bowl before I realise that, completely by accident, I've sat down next to Tony. He's looking straight ahead, ignoring me.

"All right, Tony?"

As usual, he says nothing. But at least he isn't laughing. That's something,

I suppose.

The first activity after breakfast is volcanic vent surfing. We've each been given a rubber safety suit to protect us from the heat. The others are moaning about having to wear them, but as far as I'm concerned it's a total win. At least with my suit on no one can see my spots!

Drago takes us to a clearing in the middle of the Frondy Forest. A cliff face stretches up before us. About halfway down, a huge stream of bubbling water gushes out of a volcanic vent. It travels along straight for a bit, then it's joined by the stream from another vent and

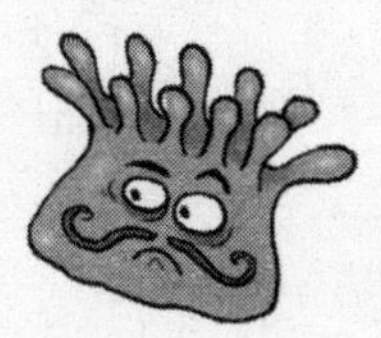

goes into a HUGE downhill, twisting and turning and even pulling up into a loop the loop. I've been volcanic vent surfing with my dad before and it's TOTALLY AWESOME.

"All right, you lot," Drago says as soon as we're ready. "It's time to surf the fear! It's time to feel the heat! It's time to – it's time to... I want you to ride the jets of hot water from the vents."

Rick and Donny go first, and are pretty quick. Tony goes second, but he obviously has a bit of bad luck and skims off course (the trick is keeping your whole body inside the current).

I decide to have another go at getting into his good books. Tucking my fins close to my body, I barrel roll down the stream, picking up speed, then use my hammer to hook Tony's tail, swing him round and put him back on course!

I finish just behind him. I grin and go for a high fin.

But my fin is left dangling in empty water. Tony has completely ignored me again!

Ralph swims over. "I dunno why you're bothering. He obviously doesn't want anything to do with you."

Ralph might have a point. My plan to impress Tony hasn't exactly worked as I hoped it would.

Soon it's time for lunch. Drago leads us into the Frondy Forest. "Right, cubs, you've all had fun vent surfing, yes?"

We all nod.

"And I bet you've worked up an appetite for lunch, right?"

Everyone nods even harder. Ralph looks at my mouth, fins his tummy and nods thirty-seven times.

"Well, there's no such thing as a free lunch out here in the wild," Drago says. "No more clamburgers and hotfrogs for you. You're going to have to find your own food. Are you with me?"

We all stop nodding and start groaning. But Drago isn't listening. "You have one hour to come back with the best feast ever! GO!!!"

We went.

We came back.

I have:

1. Three bent sea-carrots. (Ick.)
2. Half a dog-eared sea cucumber. (Double ick.)
3. Two crab-apples. (Quadruple ick, times ten.)
4. Some lobster milk I've collected in my hat. (Ewwww.)

Ralph has three brown, knobbly things that could be tide-ginger or could be sea-cowpats. He isn't sure. Joe was too scared to go into the Frondy Forest alone, so he's been relying on us to bring him back his lunch.

"Actually, I don't think I'm hungry any more," he says as soon as he sees our offerings.

"I don't think I'll ever be hungry again," I say, sniffing the could-be-tide-ginger-could-be-cowpat.

Drago starts swimming up and down in front of us. "Okay, you lot, now you've had your lunch," he says as I pour the sour lobster milk away, "it's time for the grand finale of this camp. But first, I need to put you into teams. I want Team Fearless to be scared of NOTHING, Team Awesome to be the BEST, Team Amazing to stop at nothing to WIN, Team Invincible

to be UNBEATABLE, Team Incredible to BLOW OUR MINDS and Team Supreme to come OUT ON TOP whatever happens!"

I'm not sure how all six teams can be the winner, but Drago is on such a roll I decide not to interrupt him. Drago puts me in Team Supreme along with:

1. Ralph (not bad, I suppose)
2. Joe (could be worse)
3. Donny (and so it is worse)
4. Rick (yup, worse as worse can be)
5. Tony (shall I give it one last try with him?)

Drago puffs his dogfish chest out, and swims between the teams. "This is the ultimate challenge. The one that will

stretch you all to the limit."

My mind is racing. What's it going to be this time?

"I've put you in teams because this isn't something you can do alone."

Oh, I hope it's not rock swimming. I hate rock swimming, and Joe has no jelly for heights.

"This will push you," Drago continues. "This will make you work together, and this will MAKE or BREAK you as a TEAM!!!"

Pop pop pop pop!

(That's not Joe, that's me!)

Drago waits for a second. We all

stare at him, open-mouthed. What is it going to be?

"You're going to swim a relay race!"

Oh.

Silence. From. Everyone.

Is that all? A relay race? The way Drago was going on, you'd think we were going to be scaling the north trench of Deep Everest!

Ah well, at least Rick won't be able to make me look like an idiot in a relay race.

Drago fires a bullet-fish, just like the starter in the Olimpet Stadium. The first

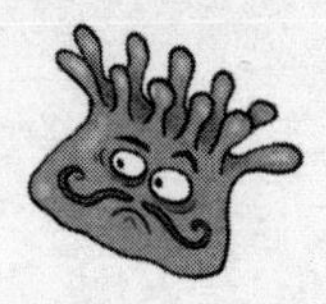

fish speed away and the race is on!

We've each got to do one lap of the camp swimming track. Joe is away first for Team Supreme. His tentacles twirl behind him like streamers and he's carrying the baton in his teeth. Ralph and I cheer him on. Rick and Donny don't seem to be that impressed at being in a team with us. Tony is floating on his own. I can't wait to see him race. I bet he'll be super fast.

"Look at him," Rick sneers as Joe falls behind teams Invincible and Amazing. "He's so slow he couldn't overtake a sea snail."

"Shut it, Rick," I say. "He's doing his best."

"Yeah, but the problem is, his best is rubbish," Rick says, squaring up to me. "Or have you SPOTTED some skills in your friend that I haven't SPOTTED?"

Donny points at my ink spots and giggles.

"At least he's trying," I say.

Rick just fins his nose at me and turns away. I look at Tony, but he's not even watching the race.

Drago is looking at his stopwatch as the teams come round the final bend. Ralph gets into position, and holds out his fin for the baton from Joe. By the time Joe passes it to him he's in fourth place.

Ralph swims off and Joe hangs, deflated, on the fence.

I try to concentrate on the race and not on Donny, who has now got a pencil and is trying to join the dots on my dorsal. Ralph zooms round the track. Pilot fish are used to keeping up with much faster species like sharks, so he's really speedy. Ralph pushes as fast as his little tail will allow. As he swims into the home straight, we've moved up a place to third!

Donny takes the baton from Ralph and the third lap begins.

"Make sure you don't drop that baton when you give it to me," Rick shouts. "Or I'll give you a biting you won't forget!"

"Wow, great way to support your team-mate," I hiss at Rick.

Rick glares at me. "I don't care about this stupid team. All I care about is getting the fastest individual lap and the medal that comes with it."

Before I can say anything, Rick moves out onto the track to wait for Donny. As Rick stretches out his fin for the baton, Donny comes around in second!

Lap four begins.

Rick zooms off with all the sleek skill of a reef shark. He's soon gaining on the bull shark from Team Invincible who's in

first place.

Even I'm impressed – but it doesn't stop me wishing that Rick was a nicer shark to everyone around him.

Rick pulls alongside the bull shark on the back straight. He flicks his tail effortlessly, nose down. **Kick, kick, kick.**

As they take the last bend, I get into place. Rick comes round in the lead. My heart starts to pound. We might actually have a chance of winning this!

I wait, my fin out, watching as Rick gets closer and closer. I kick away, knowing I'm going to have to match his speed as he reaches for me...

Closer! Closer! CLOSER! CLOSER!

The baton is almost in my grasp, and then Rick hisses at me through his sharp, gritted teeth. "The fastest lap is mine, Harry Prammer and the Spotty Hammer. Mine!"

And he drops the baton just as I reach for it! It slips through my fin, looking like it was me who dropped it!

The baton spins down. As the other cubs speed away, they stir up the silt at the bottom of the track, turning the water cloudy. The baton disappears from view.

Quickly, I flick on my hammer-vision and direct it towards the seabed.

PING!

I sense the baton! It's three metres away.

I turn and dive down.

PING!

One metre.

PING!

Fifty centimetres.

BOING!

The baton bashes into my nose and I grab for it wildly.

Grasping it tight, I do a fast 180-degree horizontal tail-kick and push off as hard as I can.

But I'm in last place.

GRRRRRRRRRRRRRRRRRR!!!!!

I am SO ANGRY at Rick. All he wants to do is spoil things for everyone. Well, Rick, you're NOT going to spoil this race for me. Camp has been a total disaster. I've been laughed at, had stupid songs sung about me, been ignored by Tony and covered in SQUID FARTS!

Well, no MORE!!

I kick and kick and kick. With each wave of my tail I imagine the water

wafting squid-fart ink all over Rick's sneery smile.

Wave. Waft! Wave. Waft! Wave. Waft! Wave. Waft!

Hahahahahahaha!

It's working! I'm GOING FASTER!!!!!

I pass Team Fearless into fifth place!

I kick and kick on, moving the baton to my teeth for extra fluid-dynamic sleekness.

I pass Team Incredible into fourth place!

On and on, just two bends to go. My tail is beginning to hurt but I keep going. The lobster from Team Awesome is

flagging and I pass him easily into third place!

One bend to go.

Wave. Waft! I picture Rick's smug face being splattered with ink.

I power past the blue-fin tuna from Team Amazing and I'm in second.

There's just the super-fast dolphin of Team Invincible left on the home straight. I can see Tony getting into position. This is your last chance, I think. If you don't want to be my friend after the lap I've just swum, you're not worth being friends with!

I kick deeper and harder than I ever

have in my life. I overtake the dolphin into first place and hold the baton out to Tony.

Tony the tiger shark.

The same breed as the fastest, bestest sharklete in the sea. We. Have. This. Race. Won!

I hand the baton over and Tony is away!

"Go on, Tony! Swim it! Leave 'em for fish food!" I scream as I clatter into Ralph and Joe, who've swum over to catch me.

Then something happens that I wasn't expecting at all.

Tony doesn't swim very fast.

Huh?

I mean – yeah, he's okay – but there's no co-ordination. His fins aren't in sequence with his tail at all. He's all over the place.

He does his best, but by the time he comes back round we're in third place.

We haven't won the race.

I don't believe it.

Tony swims in, puffing hard. He hands the baton to Joe and swims off without saying a word.

It's the official Medal Ceremony and I'm officially sulking. Camp has been rubbish. I haven't made friends with Tony and I haven't done well in a single event. All I've done is been teased and cheated and covered in spots!

Drago has made us all form a circle. He swims into the middle of it and blows his whistle loudly. I know he's got loads of medals to give out. But none of them are

for me. I close my eyes and start singing loudly in my head. Maybe if I don't see or hear any of the others winning I won't feel so bad.

"And the winner of—" Drago begins.

LA LA LA LA LA LA LA!

'And next up it's—"

LA LA LA LA LA LA LA!

"And this year's Best Newcomer is – Tony Tiger!"

Whoops. I forgot to sing. I open one eye and watch Tony collect his medal. He doesn't look very happy about it.

"But, Dad, Tony was the only newcomer," Donny whines.

"Exactly," says Drago. "So he must be the best." He turns back to the rest of us. "And now the medals for the winning team in the relay race."

LA LA LA LA LA LA LA LA LA LA LA

LA LA LA LA LA LA LA !

I shut my eyes tight and keep singing away in my head, louder and louder for what feels like forever.

LA LA LA LA LA LA LA LA LA LA LA LA LA LA LA LA LA LA !

Suddenly I feel someone nudging my side. I open my eyes and see Joe and Ralph grinning at me.

"Go on," Ralph says, pointing a fin towards Drago.

Drago is holding out a medal – to me. And he's smiling – at me.

"What's happened?" I whisper to Ralph.

"You've won Fastest Lap in the Relay," Ralph says with a grin.

"What?!" I turn to Joe. "Have I fallen asleep?" I whisper to him.

Joe looks at me like I'm crazy. "No. Why?"

I start pinching myself with my fin.

"What are you doing?" Ralph says.

"Checking I'm not dreaming." I pinch myself even harder. "Ouch!" But Drago is still there, holding a medal out to me.

I swim over to him and everyone cheers. Well, everyone apart from Rick and Donny, who are looking really, really, really annoyed.

"Well done, young Harry!" Drago says as he hangs the medal round my neck. "That was one of the BEST, FASTEST LAPS I HAVE EVER SEEN IN ALL MY YEARS AS AN OLIMPET COACH – er, I mean, sea-cub leader."

I swim back to Ralph and Joe, still in shock.

"Okay, cubs, I'm going to see if the whalecoach is ready," Drago calls. "Go and get your tents and bags."

As soon as he's gone, Rick swims over to me.

"There's no way you could have beaten me," he hisses. "I'm a reef shark. I'm one of the fastest sharks in the whole ocean."

"You're a cheat," a voice says behind me. A voice I don't recognise. I turn round and see Tony.

"What did you say?" Rick snarls.

Tony's face starts going pink. "You're a cheat," he says again. "I saw you drop

the baton on purpose when you were supposed to hand it to Harry."

I open my mouth to say something but I'm so shocked, nothing comes out.

"That's how I know he can't have been faster than me," Rick says. "That's exactly why I dropped it – so that he wouldn't beat me!"

"YOU DROPPED THE BATON ON PURPOSE?" We all jump at the sound of Drago's voice. He's swum up right behind us and he's looking really mad.

"I – er – well – I..." Rick splutters.

"Right, you and Donny are sitting by me on the coach so I can teach you all

about the importance of teamwork – ALL THE WAY HOME!"

"Dad!" Donny whinges.

"B-but— " Rick splutters.

"No buts!" Drago says. "Come on, cubs, let's get going."

As everyone swims off, I turn back to Tony. "Hey, thanks for standing up for me with Rick."

Tony's face goes even pinker. He looks really

embarrassed. "That's okay. I should have said something sooner – when I saw him drop the baton, but..." He looks away.

"Are you all right?" I say.

Tony nods. "I'm rubbish at talking when I don't know anyone. I get really shy. I think people are going to make fun of me so I just stay quiet."

I stare at him. "Really? I thought you didn't like me because – because I'm a hammerhead."

"No way!" Tony says, and he starts to grin. "I think you're ace. And your lap was awesome! I wish I could swim as fast as you."

I feel like I'm dreaming all over again.

Tony looks at me. "D-do you want to sit next to me on the coach?"

I must have looked really shocked, because Tony's eyes drop. "It's okay if you don't want to. Don't worry. Bad idea. Sorry."

"No!" I say quickly. "I'd love to sit next to you."

This is totally brilliant!

"So you want to be friends?" I say, just to check I'm not imagining it.

Tony nods. "Yes, please."

I swim up for a high-fin and this time

Tony high-fins me right back!

The coach is packed and we're all inside. I sit next to Tony on the back seats right behind Ralph and Joe. Rick and Donny are up at the front with Drago. He's giving them a long talk about the "SEVEN HUNDRED ways to be the BEST TEAM PLAYER EVER".

What a brilliant end to the camp!

And then I realise that I've achieved everything in my plan.

1. I'm friends with Tony the Tiger. Tick!
2. I'm the fastest sharklete in the sea-cubs. Tick!

3. Rick and Donny are sitting in complete silence next to Drago. Tick! Tick! Tick!
4. Things don't get much better than this!